Single Voice

1 book | 2 stories

Single Voice

1 BOOK flip 2 STORIES

Will Julie face the truth about her brother?

Nadia Xerri-L.

just julie

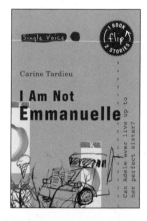

Single Voice

1 BOOK flip 2 STORIES

Carine Tardieu

I Am Not Emmanuelle

Can Adele ever live up to her perfect sister?

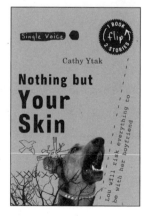

Single Voice

1 BOOK flip 2 STORIES

Cathy Ytak

Nothing but Your Skin

Lou will risk everything to be with her boyfriend

Single Voice

1 BOOK flip 2 STORIES

Gilles Abier

The Pool Was Empty

Celia says it was an accident, but that's not what Alex's mother saw

Single Voice

Jean-Philippe Blondel

A Place to Live

annick press
toronto + new york + vancouver

First published in France as *Un endroit pour vivre*, ©Actes Sud, 2007
English translation ©2009 Annick Press

Series editor: Melanie Little

Translated by Paula Ayer
Copyedited by Geri Rowlatt
Proofread by Helen Godolphin
Cover design by David Drummond/Salamander Hill Design
Interior design by Monica Charny
Cover photo ©Shutterstock

*To J.-L. Guillaume, O. Bigeard, and V. May. To my colleagues. To my students, past
and present, particularly to the T euros 06/07. To U.V. and A.K.*

We acknowledge the support of the Canada Council for the Arts, the Ontario
Arts Council, and the Government of Canada through the Book Publishing
Industry Development Program (BPIDP) for our publishing activities.

ONTARIO ARTS COUNCIL
CONSEIL DES ARTS DE L'ONTARIO

FSC
Mixed Sources
Cert no. SW-COC-00127
© 1996 FSC

Annick Press is committed to protecting our natural
environment. As part of our efforts, the text of this
book is printed on 100% post-consumer recycled
fibers.

Printed and bound in Canada by Friesens.

Published in the U.S.A. by	Distributed in Canada by	Distributed in the U.S.A. by
Annick Press (U.S.) Ltd.	Firefly Books Ltd.	Firefly Books (U.S.) Inc.
	66 Leek Crescent	P.O. Box 1338
	Richmond Hill, ON	Ellicott Station
	L4B 1H1	Buffalo, NY 14205

Visit our website at www.annickpress.com

It's all because of the new principal,
Mr. Langley—tall and thin as a rake.

Because of his speeches.

Because of his way of stressing all
the negative words when he talks: *do
not*, *forbidden*, *never*, *no one*.

Because of the way they all looked at
him—like sheep. Moist eyes, glazed-

over expressions. Obedient. Tamed. It ate me up.

But I never talked about it to anyone.

But then, I don't talk about much to anyone—except for Evan, sometimes. Maybe that's why people at school like me: I'm a guy without baggage. I haven't failed or skipped a grade; I'm not good or bad; I'm not the best student or the worst. I'm just in the middle. I get invited to parties, and I go once in a while. I let people copy my homework and don't ask for anything in return. I stay cool. I moved

here from the other side of the
country last year, near the end of the
semester—my dad got a job transfer
—so no one really knows me yet.
But they like me. Girls have started
to hang around me. They're nice to
me. They say I understand them.
They've convinced themselves that
I'm sensitive, even though they have
no reason to think that. I never reveal
anything. I know how to keep my
mouth shut. And how to observe
people. That's what I like most of
all—observing.

I watch women in the street get

angry when their husbands aren't listening to them. I see the disappointed faces of mothers whose children don't need them anymore. I notice how guys and girls try to get each other's attention when spring is coming—shorter skirts, tighter pants, thin T-shirts showing off muscles. I can spend hours just watching the world.

My mother always nagged me about it when I was younger. "Stop daydreaming," she'd say. It was like her motto. My mother thinks you should always be doing something. Because my dad's at work all the time, she complains that she has to work twice as hard—first at the office, then at home. Obviously, it's not true—not for the last few years, anyway, because I help her out a lot. But she'll never admit it. She really loves to complain. Complaining makes her feel alive.

My mom's a secretary. At the beginning of my first year in junior high, she told me the teachers would need to get information about our family, and I'd have to fill out some forms. "On the forms, there'll be a spot where it asks about your parents' profession," she said, and then she told me it was very important to put down that she was an *executive secretary*.

My mother has never been an executive secretary.

She's tried hard enough, though.

Once, on a job interview, she even tried to pass herself off as trilingual —English, French, and German— even though she can't say two words in a foreign language without laughing.

But, as she never stops repeating,
nothing ventured, nothing gained.

My mom is a cliché factory.

She just slides them onto the end of
every sentence, effortlessly. It's like
they wait in her mouth, hiding, and
at the last moment they spring on
her helpless victim: *A bird in the hand
is worth two in the bush. Don't count
your chickens before they hatch. April
showers bring May flowers.*

Except right now, it's April and there
aren't any showers. And life is too
complicated for clichés.

For two weeks now, it's been really warm. Abnormally warm for April— though who knows what normal is anymore. On the radio, they go on and on about seasonal norms, but what does that mean? Most of us just try to enjoy the weather while it lasts, without thinking too much about what it means. We live for the moment, even though we know the planet is being destroyed and, sooner or later, we'll have to deal with it.

I'm sixteen.

I'm in my last year of school.

In sixteen years times three, the scientists say, Earth will be a very different place. The planet we know today will be just a distant memory.

I already miss it.

Sometimes, before I fall asleep, I imagine myself in three or four decades. Shut up inside a stifling house, unable to go outside because of the brutal heat of the sun. I'm lying on a dirty mattress, waiting for darkness to bring relief. When night falls, the humans go outside. They breathe in the air. They kiss and make love and fight. Sometimes they kill each other. Human contact has become urgent. I spend all day lying in bed, flipping through the novels I've rescued from people who don't want them—people who say books are *frivolous*, who say now that we have science, we don't need fiction.

I daydream.

And my mother's not there to reprimand me.

My mother is lying under a tombstone that she had inscribed to read *Executive Secretary*.

I got into books early.

Or more like I was pushed into them.

By my mother's constant busyness and my father's absence. By their need to be alone together whenever they had time.

I figured it out quickly—what they wanted from me, most of all, was to "not get in the way" and to "play with friends my own age." I learned to keep a low profile. I also learned that reading helped. All of a sudden I could be someone else. Live another life. Or, even better, invent one.

I thought about becoming a writer, but my grades in English weren't too encouraging. A writer with red marks all over his papers, a writer who doesn't know how to use the pluperfect or what a conjunction is or how to structure an essay—yeah, that would be impressive. Not to mention that my spelling isn't great, either. At one of the parent-teacher interviews, the English teacher told me I should read more. Even my mom was surprised.

She said, "But he never stops reading."
And the teacher smiled and said,
"No, I mean something besides
comic books and manga." My mom
nodded. So did I. What else was I
supposed to do?

I never read manga. I don't read
many comics.

I tried—I just couldn't get into them.

So I quit books and went straight
into movies.

My mother didn't notice much of a
change, except in her wallet. Going

to the movies is expensive. She asked me why I didn't just rent movies. I shrugged. It's not that hard to figure out—the sensation of walking into the theater, the whispers, the anticipation that in ten minutes, the world outside will disappear like magic— but she wouldn't have understood. She thinks watching movies at home is so much more convenient, because you can press pause to go to the bathroom. And it's so much more comfortable to be in your own home.

Home, sweet home.

The early bird gets the worm.

Never say never.

In the spring, a young man's fancy turns to thoughts of love.

No, she doesn't like that one.

The principal wouldn't like it either, no doubt.

Spring is too hot; there are no April showers. And he can't compete with spring. That puts him in a bad mood.

▬▬▬ ●

He arrived in September. He's an autumn kind of guy.

I didn't know the old principal. Apparently, he was a little old grandpa who quietly whiled away the hours until his retirement, trying to take it easy and showing his face as little as possible. The school functioned without him; the vice principals and teachers kept things running. Grandpa signed the report cards at the end of the term and fell asleep sometimes in staff meetings. Grandpa didn't like conflict, either, so as soon as a parent would get mad about something, he'd give in. He'd say to his secretary that, in the end, there wasn't much he could do. If a failing student was promoted to the next year even though he shouldn't have been, it was really the parents' problem, not the school's. It wasn't going to change the world. Then he'd close the door to his office and sit back down at his computer to play solitaire. He loved his solitaire.

I know all that because of Evan.

Evan's mom is one of the school's vice principals. It's not easy for him at school, but he deals with it. He says that it's better than being the son of an undertaker or an arms dealer. Sometimes we make a list of jobs we don't want to do when we're older: slaughterhouse worker, fish-monger, telemarketer, guy who holds up the "applause" sign on TV shows. It's way easier than thinking of jobs we actually want to do.

Evan's also one of our class reps—Evan and Marion. Everyone knew those two would be elected. Good students, responsible, not suck-ups. And they know how to speak in public without turning the color of a tomato, though they still blush just a little because they take it seriously. When a debate falls flat in English or history class, they're always the ones to bring it back to life.

For a while, everyone was betting they'd start dating. But nothing came of it. Marion's seeing a guy who goes to another school, and Evan's been single since he broke up with Lily.

And ever since then, I've been seeing more of him. First, it was just because we had stuff to work on together. I was elected as the deputy representative. I'm supposed to replace him on student council meetings if he's away sick—even though I know he'll never be away sick.

I was sitting in the desk behind him the day of the vote. At the start of class, he turned around, looked me in the eyes, and said, "You want to be a team?" I was so surprised—he had never really spoken to me before— that I said yes. My name and his. It was strange to see them together on the blackboard. And even stranger to see the votes piling up underneath them. Evan is really popular, and no one has a problem with me. We got elected in a landslide. When I walked out of class, I was still stunned. Everyone was patting me on the back, congratulating me, even though I knew I'd done nothing to deserve it. But, for the first time, I said to myself that maybe I really could enjoy it here. Maybe the school could be my anchor. Not just a place to go—a place to live.

So Evan and I got together a few times, to talk about the candidates for the social committee and the plans to improve the school. We thought about starting a film club but realized right away that no one but us would be interested. That's when we started having more serious conversations. Evan's really into movies, too, but not the same ones as me. He likes American movies, and I'm into European and Asian ones. He likes action. I'm more contemplative.

I like to daydream.

I went to Evan's place once, but I felt weird there. His house is right behind the school and it felt like I was at school on my day off. I couldn't figure out how he could stand it.

Evan and I may be friends, but I don't know much about him.

We're not together all the time, and sometimes three or four days go by and we don't talk except to say hi. I text message other people in my class way more often and I visit their blogs all the time. Evan's more elusive. I know he has a blog, but he's never given me the address. It's not a big deal; that's just the way he is. And anyway, I have no choice—it's not like I have a lot of close friends.

Evan never says anything about the new principal.

Sometimes he criticizes the teachers or makes fun of the associate principal's beer belly, but as for the principal—nothing. I mentioned it to him once. He raised his eyebrows. He said he had to watch what he said or else his mom could get in trouble. So he stuck with *no comment*—and that's all he would say. It wasn't the same thing with the teachers or the associate principal—they're his mom's colleagues. The principal is a boss. He's *the* boss.

I remember rolling my eyes when he told me that. I said, "What is this, the 1950s?" Evan said that nothing had really changed since then, had it? I thought about my father—always away from home, the nights he spent in motels with other sales reps, in some depressing town in the middle of nowhere. I thought about my mom and her obsession with being an executive secretary. I remember being jealous of Evan when we discussed economics and history in class because he always knew what he was talking about—he knew what he stood for. As for me, I wasn't so sure. I knew I had a struggle—but I wasn't sure if I had what it takes to win.

At the time, I didn't know I was so close to proving that I did. Or that all the actors were already there, under my nose. Under the April sun—the sun that was causing skirts to shorten and heads to turn. The sun that was driving the principal crazy—Charles Langley, fifty-six years old, the master of the house.

The week before, he had given detention to two juniors for kissing "flagrantly" in the hall. On Tuesday, he sent a kid home just for wearing shorts, because pants should come down to the ankles... *This is not a place where anything goes.*

And then yesterday—the last straw.

Or maybe it was the first.

The spark that lit the fire, anyway.

The big speech.

All the class reps and their deputies
were there.

I was sitting between Marion and
Evan. Marion was frowning and
fanning herself with her notebook. It

was hot in the room. The sun burned through the windows. Evan was biting his lip. Once, he started to say something to me, then changed his mind. He said it wasn't important. I could see something was bothering him and was about to say something when Langley walked in, accompanied by the entire administrative staff.

They sat behind the tables set up at the front. Evan's mother stared at the far wall. She clenched her jaw. The associate principal flipped through his papers. Langley's eyes shot daggers at us.

And then, it began.

No preamble.

It felt like a debriefing in a cop show.
*We're looking for the killer; what evidence
do we have? The mayor wants imme-
diate results. We need to make an arrest,
and quick.*

First he said that school was not
supposed to be an amusement park.
He let out a sharp little laugh. No
one reacted. He cleared his throat.

Then he said that we had to remind

ourselves, and remind everyone else, that school was, above all, a place of work. He had a bunch of charts and graphs that he pointed to while he was talking—pies, bars, lines, and curves of red and blue and green. My head was spinning. He recited numbers and percentages. He said he had come to the definitive conclusion that the recent downward trend in exam results was due to the increasingly lax atmosphere in the school and to the fact that our common goals as students had been forgotten. *You all need to learn the values of dignity, respect, and hard work.* I couldn't believe my ears. Even my grandmother wouldn't have said something like that.

So, in short, it was time to put some structure back into the school.

Rigid smile.

Dead silence.

I heard an ambulance siren outside on the street. Someone was in pain somewhere. Someone would be calling someone else to say, quietly, "There's been an accident. You have to come."

Then came the avalanche of rules—

agreed to by a majority of the parents, he said. Impeccable dress at all times, no sitting in the hall, no hanging around the school building, absolutely no "canoodling"—that's the word he used—on the benches, on the lawn, anywhere on school property. It was time to return to the key principles of success: work, discipline, and consequences.

The moral of his story was: school is a place to *work*.

━━ ●

I've never really understood the dif-
ference between life and work.

People talk about them like they're
opposites, and I don't see why. The
few friends my parents have are people they work with. A lot of couples
meet at work. Love is something you
can work on, and friendship, too.
Work is life, and life is work, isn't it?

What killed me about it all was the
way the others reacted.

When we got back to our class, we
had to repeat Principal Langley's
sermon to them. That's why we're

there, the class reps and the deputies—to balance good and bad news.

I thought there would have been a reaction, an outcry, calls to start a petition or to march in protest. But nothing. Just a few annoyed-looking pouts and some disbelieving expressions.

I told myself that they needed time to absorb the shock. That they'd shake themselves into action the next day, or the day after. But the next day and the day after, there was still nothing. Joris and Sonia had stopped kissing on the second-floor landing. Lisa and Sam had stopped sitting outside together on the grass.

It made me sick, really.

For days, I couldn't think about anything else. I handed in a blank exam in history class. The teacher raised his eyebrows; I had never done that before. He asked for an explanation, and I just shrugged. What could I say? That I didn't want to exist in a place where we weren't allowed to live?

And then there was English class.

We were discussing a story that talked about the power of images, and the teacher asked us, on the spot, to say what our favorite movie was, and why. I saw all the answers projected in my head—faces, directors' names, scenes. I go to the movies twice a week; sometimes it's like I'm living two lives, one on screen and the other where I get up every morning and go to school. When the teacher got around to me, though, I just mumbled something incoherent. I couldn't think of anything intelligent to say. She was surprised. She reminded me that at the beginning of the year, I'd said I wanted to become a film director. I turned red. I lowered my eyes.

Then, all of a sudden, I opened them.

All of a sudden, everything was clear. I knew what I had to do.

I had a mission.

I didn't listen to anything that happened for the rest of the class. Or in the next class. Or for the rest of that day.

Everything was falling into place— quietly, slowly.

━━ ●

The next day, I came to school with my dad's camcorder. He bought it because everyone else was buying them, but he doesn't even know how to work it. When my parents weren't around, I taught myself how to use it, and now I'm an expert.

I would have to explain myself carefully.

If I didn't, everyone would think I was a pervert, a voyeur—they'd turn me in to the principal, or even to the cops.

But actually, it wasn't as hard as I thought.

You have to have faith in humanity sometimes.

Because it turned out that everyone was shocked by the principal's new rules— they just didn't know what to do about it.

My camcorder and I would be the choreographers.

I started with Joris and Sonia. They would be my inspiration.

They were already together when they started high school. They've known each other since kinder-garten. They've been kissing since elementary school.

So they had no objection.

And they didn't even need to pretend.

They kissed—in front of me.

On camera.

Long, wet, soft, intense, sweet.

I watched them. I was fascinated by their skin. By the way Sonia pressed into her man. I got a lump in my throat. I wondered if anyone had ever wanted me that way.

Obviously, the answer was no.

Sure, I've had a few girlfriends.

Nothing serious. While some science teacher was talking about atoms, I'd roll up a note into a ball and throw it to the other side of the class, and the replies would land in my pencil case. *I think you're cute. We should go out. Meet outside the school at 5, ok?* I was in grade six.

Then technology entered the picture. I'd get texts on my phone between classes. *Someone likes u. Can u guess who?* Abbreviations, emoticons, cookie-cutter sentences. I'm not making fun of it—I wrote them, too.

Except...

Except it never lasted long.

I'd always get dumped.

Always nicely.

I'm not someone you want to hurt.

It's just that—there was no "chemistry."

One girl, Laura Green, told me it was a relief when we stopped going out together. It was "too weird" dating me, apparently. It was like I wasn't there. Like I was in my head, just observing, instead of doing something, making a move. "You would daydream and daydream, and I just kept waiting for you to snap out of it and kiss me already," she told me. I couldn't help laughing—she did, too. We're still on good terms. I'm on good terms with all my exes. It feels stupid to call them "exes," though. Ex-whats? Anyway, it doesn't matter—they all live in another city now.

Ever since I came here last year, I've had no luck with girls at all.

━━ ●

What's for sure is that I've never experienced anything like this. Hearts beating wildly, the smell of each other's skin, bodies calling to each other, with all their strength, with all their weakness—a kiss. *I don't know who I am when you're not with me.* Another kiss. Forgetting the world outside.

I've never been Joris. I've never been Sonia.

Those two were my first. I filmed them behind the cafeteria building, on the grass. It was 1:35 in the afternoon. There was no one around except us.

I know it might seem weird. I know it might seem perverted. But actually, it was one of the most beautiful moments of my life.

When it was over, the three of us held hands. They were a little red-faced, and so was I.

▬▬● ●

My cheeks were still flushed when I got to class and sat down next to Evan, breathless. He whispered, "What have *you* been doing?"

"Nothing. I'll tell you later."

He nodded and said that whatever it was, it suited me. I asked him what he was talking about, but he just smiled.

All through class, I couldn't stop staring at the Spanish teacher's lips. I wondered if there was someone, somewhere, waiting for her.

The next day, I went outside with Lisa and Sam.

Lisa and Sam are in my class. They've just started going out. They're low-key—they don't make waves. He's not a very good student, and she's one of the best. She's an overachiever and he's always flunking. They know that a lot of people say they won't last. But already, you can see the connection between them. When they have a problem, they face it together. It doesn't scare them.

Still, I wasn't sure how they'd react to my plan.

Lisa was tying her shoes while I told them about my project. I started out very clear and calm, but when they didn't say anything, I came undone. I started searching for words and mumbling. Then Lisa lifted her head and said, "Okay, we'll do it, but just him in my arms."

I wasn't sure exactly what she meant, but I was so surprised she agreed to it that I said yes, for sure.

They sat against the wall of the main building, in the April sunshine.

He put his head on her shoulder.

She stroked the nape of his neck, gently and rhythmically. I shot a close-up of her hand and his neck. A light breeze ruffled his hair.

It took my breath away.

It happened little by little. I held the camera, transfixed by the two of them. Lisa stroking him, calming, reassuring. Sam's head lifting toward her. Her finger tracing the outline of his left ear—so delicate and fragile —and her hands like a whisper—*I'm here, it's okay, I'm here*. I felt a tingle just above my belly button. It slithered up my chest like a snake and coiled

in my neck. My eyes filled with tears.
I could have held them back by
looking up at the sky—the serenely
blue April sky—but I couldn't look
away, or maybe I didn't want to. I
stayed there, watching the little moving
square, watching Lisa's hands and
Sam's hair, and letting my tears flow.

When we were done—when they
saw the tears running down my
cheeks—Lisa came up to me. Sam,
too. They hugged me for a long time,
without saying a word. And then we
pulled apart.

I knew their bodies had left a mark

on my skin. And I knew from then on, they'd stand by me, right to the end.

After that, word got around.

There's someone at school who... Do you know the guy who...? What do you think of the...?

So I didn't have to look for my subjects anymore.

I was scared that the principal would hear the rumors. But I told Evan about it, and he made sure everyone honored the code of silence. He didn't say a word to his mother, even though she wouldn't have done anything to discourage me. He said it was *our* business, not hers. He emphasized the word "ours." I felt supported.

Supported.

Carried.

Carried away.

They came to see me with their ideas. No special effects, no staging, no acting—just natural lighting and ordinary gestures, captured on film.

There was Finn and Matilda. He held her face in his hands and they just looked at each other, not even smiling. It was as if they were drowning and saving each other at the same time.

Then, Ellen and Mosef. The two of them rode across the parking lot on her bike, his head resting on her shoulder. I thought Mosef wouldn't want to do it. He said, "Well, you're wrong! My mom would be super excited if she knew I was in a movie. Even a movie like this." He laughed, a booming laugh, and then Ellen started laughing. They had a really hard time being serious after that.

And Mya and Michael, behind the fence, sitting on a low wall. They held hands. They closed their eyes and let the sunshine flood over them. A moment of peace in a world of conflict. A forbidden interlude.

Love.

The most overused, insignificant, abused, invincible word.

Love in every color, every way, every shape.

And me—my hand steady, my eyes riveted to the scene—detached, but extremely present.

And then, my project expanded.

▬▬●

It was a Thursday morning.

The English teacher tore into the computer lab at full speed, glanced around, sat down next to me, looked me straight in the eyes, and said, "It's too simple. You're not the only ones in this school. And not everything is about love. There's hate, suffering, bravery, kindness—you need to show all of it." She stood up and left the room without turning around.

I was blown away. All of a sudden, my project took on a larger meaning. I felt dizzy, but at the same time, I understood what she wanted to say.

━━ •

So, I picked up the pace.

After class, the teacher lecturing two students she had held back. Speaking with her hands, her fingers flying up in the air and descending again, frenzied.

In the hallway, the juniors studying
for their big math test. Elise walking
up and down the hall, reciting magic
formulas.

In the courtyard, Alice and Peter,
breaking up. Her running away,
waving her hands furiously to stop
herself from crying. In the custodians'
room, people erupting in laughter.

In front of the cafeteria, two boys
and a girl improvising a dance, with
their friends around them, clapping.

Someone coming out of the teachers'
lounge, slamming the door. Through

the crack, a glimpse of the coffee machine and Pascale W. smiling. In the bathrooms, a little farther away, the sound of muffled sobs. And then the bell ringing and everyone scattering like a spooked herd of cattle.

On the second floor, Jeff P. and Jeff C. fighting, almost coming to blows. Emily running toward them, furious, screaming even louder than them, making them go quiet.

And as I watch it all, nobody pays attention to me. I hide my camera.

━━ ●

People are starting to say hi to me in the morning. More than they did before.

When I pass in front of the fence, there are smiles, nods—signs of recognition. But the girls who used to hang around me have stopped. They watch me, a little nervous, a little puzzled.

Back at home, I edit the movie. It's how I spend all my time. I cut and insert and rearrange.

One moment, then another.

Joris and Sonia's kiss, Alice and Peter breaking up, the teacher talking to the students after class, Ellen and Mosef laughing.

One after the other, and one moment dissolves into the next.

I was afraid they wouldn't go together, but I was wrong.

Five minutes and thirty seconds of life.

If I only had an hour to live and had one last wish, I'd ask to watch those five minutes and thirty seconds again.

Even if I was forty. Even if I was sixty or a hundred.

For a long time, I couldn't decide what to do about the soundtrack. I couldn't decide because with music, it's all about different groups and scenes. One person's taste totally excludes another's. Music doesn't bring people together—it divides them. It turns them into cliques.

Even jazz. Even classical. *Especially* classical.

So I decided on silence.

A deafening silence.

I cut out all the sounds, then recorded the sound of my breath and the sound of my heart beating.

Five minutes and thirty seconds of life.

The final product.

I played it on a loop on my computer, over and over—I couldn't look away. I felt waves passing through me, getting stronger. I felt like the ground was shaking. I never realized, before I made this film, how much all these people were a part of me.

I burned a copy for the English
teacher, another one for the Spanish
teacher. And one for Marion, and
one for Evan, too.

Evan came with me yesterday to film
the final scene—where Clement
comes out of the school and down
the steps and Selena runs after him.
She's about to put her hands over his
eyes when he turns around, and
they're face to face, lips to lips. It's
the end of the day, but the sun is still
shining brightly.

I expected Evan to make fun of me,
to make some sarcastic remark. To say

it was sappy, or shallow. There was plenty of stuff to attack, but it never stopped me. I just had to keep going.

But Evan didn't say anything last night. He just watched. And he took off before I could get my things together. Clement and Selena were already far away. I was alone in the courtyard. I felt at peace, and at war. Alone, and connected. I'd never felt so connected to other people before. I'd never felt so alone before.

The next afternoon, Evan called me. He had just watched the film. He said, "Something's missing."

"What?"

"You. You're not in it anywhere."

"I'm behind the camera."

"I have an idea for a final scene. Can you meet me?"

We met in the school parking lot. It was deserted. It was Sunday, 5:40 p.m. The date and time were displayed on the screen.

Evan set up the camera.

He positioned it so I was in the frame.

He said, "Don't move."

He started filming and then, suddenly, he left the camera running and walked over to me. He came closer and closer. His breath on my neck. My heart beating. My breathing getting faster.

And the kiss.

▬▬▬ ●

Tuesday.

I'm standing in front of the principal's office. The door is closed. It's 3:00 p.m. I've been waiting half an hour.

Yeah, I'm a little scared.

But I'm ready for it.

I know I'll be expelled.

I'll get what's coming to me.

The new version, the one with the final scene, made the rounds. The English teacher showed it in class. A physics teacher did, too. The Spanish teacher kept giving me little half smiles—I couldn't tell if they were meant to be ironic. The blogs went crazy. I found out it was forbidden to film on school property without obtaining permission first. Actually, I'd known that before, but nothing was going to stop me.

I heard that the principal was hysterical.

He wanted to punish "the ringleaders" —but there was just me.

I'm not a ringleader.

I'm just a transcriber. A secretary. That's it—an *executive* secretary. I just recorded what was already there.

I was summoned earlier this afternoon. *To the office, immediately.* A teacher came with me. He's waiting with me. He says it will be okay. I say it doesn't matter.

I have no regrets.

I'm not ashamed.

I feel freer and prouder than I've ever felt.

The teacher goes to the window to look outside.

He comes back toward me. He's trying to hide a smile. He says, "They're all down in the courtyard." I don't understand what he's saying. He takes my arm and leads me to the window. "Look!"

Look at them.

All of them. Every class, every grade.

Sitting on the pavement. In the unusually warm April sun. Looking up at the principal's office.

Calm, determined.

They're occupying their territory— their place to live.

Ours.

●

Single Voice

1 book | 2 stories

Also available in the Single Voice series

Two heart-wrenching tales of sibling secrets, loyalty and loss.

JUST JULIE
Julie's idolized older brother is about to be tried for murder…and what she knows about the crime could change her life forever.

I AM NOT EMMANUELLE
Stealing a pack of gum launches Adele into a funny, poignant monologue about her many flaws—the worst of which is that she'll never measure up to her perfect, dead sister.

Two fearless explorations of the depths of teenage passion.

NOTHING BUT YOUR SKIN
Lou is obsessed with colors; her parents call her "slow" and say she can't make up her mind. But she knows she wants to be with her boyfriend—no matter what.

THE POOL WAS EMPTY
Celia is accused of murder after her boyfriend falls into an empty pool, and the shocking events of that fateful day may not be what they seem.

Vincent Karle

Descent
into
Paradise

First published in France as *Un clandestin aux Paradis*, ©Actes Sud, 2009
English translation © 2009 Annick Press

Annick Press Ltd.

Series editor: Melanie Little

Translated by Paula Ayer
Copyedited by Geri Rowlatt
Proofread by Helen Godolphin
Cover design by David Drummond/Salamander Hill Design
Interior design by Monica Charny
Cover photo ©2009 JupiterImages Corporation

For Lauriane and Aurélien, so that one day this story won't be theirs.

We acknowledge the support of the Canada Council for the Arts, the Ontario
Arts Council, and the Government of Canada through the Book Publishing
Industry Development Program (BPIDP) for our publishing activities.

Cataloging in Publication

Karle, Vincent
    Descent into paradise / Vincent Karle.

(Single voice series)
Translations of: Un clandestin aux Paradis and Un endroit pour vivre.
Title on added t.p., inverted: A place to live / Jean-Philippe Blondel.
ISBN 978-1-55451-235-5 (pbk.).—ISBN 978-1-55451-240-9 (bound)

    I. Blondel, Jean-Philippe, 1964- II. Blondel, Jean-Philippe, 1964- .
A place to live. III. Title. IV. Series: Single voice series

PZ7.K1448De 2010   j843'.92   C2009-906438-3

Published in the U.S.A. by Annick Press (U.S.) Ltd.	**Distributed in Canada by** Firefly Books Ltd. 66 Leek Crescent Richmond Hill, ON L4B 1H1	**Distributed in the U.S.A. by** Firefly Books (U.S.) Inc. P.O. Box 1338 Ellicott Station Buffalo, NY 14205

Visit our website at www.annickpress.com

It's my fault.

What happened—I didn't want it to, but it happened anyway, and now it's too late to fix it.

They came to look for me, but it was him they took away, and I'm still here.

Now I'm alone. As for him—I don't know where he is.

▬● ▬● ▬●

His name is Zaher.

That's Afghani.

My name's Martin.

At first, I didn't like him.

It's not that he wasn't cool, it's not
that he was foreign; it's just that nobody knew him. He came to Paradise
after the school year had started. He
looked like he'd just gotten off the
boat from Afghanistan—people said
that his family had fled the war. He

ended up in our class, and he had a
sister who went to the kindergarten
next door.

Afghanistan, that's Bin Laden's bud-
dies who blew up the towers in New
York, so we didn't trust him—I
mean, that's normal. I nicknamed
him "Taliban." It's a word you hear
all the time on TV. He didn't say
anything—well, he didn't understand
much—but "Taliban," he seemed to
understand that and it really pissed
him off, which just made me keep
going.

He wore a sort of brown, woollen

hat that looked like a pie plate turned over onto his head, and we never stopped teasing him about it. He only took it off in class, and underneath it he had a small cap, a bit like the skullcap that Jews wear, except yellow. The first day he talked to the teacher about it. I'm not sure how the teacher understood him, but he let him keep his cap, even though the rest of us have to take off our ball caps or else he makes a huge deal and won't start the class.

▬▬ •

A few weeks after he got here, we had a fight.

I had just taken his pie hat from him and I put it on, laughing, "Hey, look, I'm a Taliban!" He threw himself on me. He had learned a bit of English by then and he screamed, "The Taliban killed my grandfather, if you call me Taliban one more time I'll kill you!" Christ, he was crazy; it took two teachers to pull us apart! He was crying and shouting in his language.

The whole class was staring at us and nobody said anything. They looked at him silently, as if what he

said about his grandfather had changed things. I hated him for that. My grandfather died at war, too, but I don't go crying about it. I hated him, but I didn't call him Taliban anymore.

We sulked around each other for a while, but it started to bug me because bit by bit all the others were becoming friends with him. I had to admit that he knew how to get by; he learned quickly and his English kept getting better and better. Also, he didn't seem to hold a grudge against me. So I told myself that I had just been messing with him earlier.

Afghanistan is also where hashish comes from, so we all figured he must be a dealer. One night when we were waiting for the bus, I offered him a drag of my cigarette. When I saw how he inhaled it, I could tell that he had never even smoked before! I laughed at him, but he knew it wasn't mean; he laughed, too. So right there, we agreed that we could at least talk to each other, especially since he didn't live far from me and we usually walked the same way to school.

We listened to the same music—I had no idea they even knew what

reggae was in Afghanistan. We'd turn up the volume on our cellphones on the bus, the old people would quickly move away, and we'd spread out on the seats. He really had a gift for languages: English, French, Spanish; shit, in three months he had caught up to the rest of us! He even helped me with my homework.

I showed him my camera. I like taking pictures; I always have my camera on me. It was a present from my parents when I turned fifteen. Zaher had never seen one like it, and he wanted to know how it worked.

It's got tons of memory, so I can take as many shots as I like. I shoot everything in sight: my friends, the school, my family. I especially like shooting things that aren't that interesting but that catch my eye, like a ray of sunlight hitting an empty bus seat in the morning. *Click*, the ray of sunlight. *Click*, a cloud shaped like a bone. *Click*, a girl's ear with six piercings, seen from behind. I can't help myself; I don't think about it, I just shoot, that's it.

At night on my bed, I look at all of the photos I took that day, but when I see them after the fact, I think they're

lame. I don't remember anymore why I took them—they don't interest me. I don't know why, but it happens every time. It bugs me that I spent so much time taking pictures and I didn't end up with even one good one. I'm always disappointed. I should expect it by now, but every time it makes me angry and I erase them all.

Zaher taught us some words in his language. When we want to talk to each other without anyone else understanding, we speak in Pashtun.

"*Tchetôr astin*, how's it going?" "*Khub astin*, it's all good?" His hat is called a *pakol*. I have to admit, it limits conversations because we only know how to say a few things. Swear words are the easiest to remember, though.

One day I took a picture of his *pakol*, which was sitting on a chair. He wanted to see it on the screen; he laughed when he saw it, and then put the hat on my head. He laughed even more and wanted to take my photo. I gave him my camera, and after that I took a picture of him in his yellow cap. I knew then he had forgiven me for good.

Those photos—for the first time, I didn't erase them. I had them printed and then gave him both of them, his and mine. It's not that they weren't terrible, but hey, I kind of liked them.

Later I asked him, "Why don't you ever take off your cap?" He looked at me for a long time, not saying anything. Then he checked to see if anyone was looking, and lifted up his cap quickly: on one side of his head, his scalp was all burned.

━━ •

It was just before winter holidays.

We were in class with Mr. Lopez, talking about Baghdad.

Mr. Lopez is our history teacher. What's great about Mr. Lopez is that he tells us about history like it's a story. Often he goes off on tangents that aren't even in the curriculum, but we learn lots of stuff anyway, that's what's cool.

He's our favorite teacher because we can talk about anything with him; he's always ready to listen when we have questions. We have a lot of

laughs with him, but there's no messing around. When you get on his nerves, he gets really pissed off. One day, I was joking around in class while he was talking, and I got myself four hours of detention.

Right now, we're doing the Middle East; it's not in the curriculum, but Mr. Lopez says it's more important because they report on it all the time in the news and they say all sorts of misleading things. He's the only teacher who talks to us about TV; he says, "If you watch it, at least watch it critically. Listen carefully to the

information, and then verify it on your own." Anyway, we covered the whole curriculum in the first part of the semester and we had nothing else to do, so now we're all becoming experts on Iraq and Pakistan.

When we talk about Afghanistan, we have Zaher to correct the news reports on TV. Some mornings, Mr. Lopez doesn't even open our history book at the start of class; instead, he says, "So, you all saw the report on Kabul last night? Who wants to summarize it for us?" And then, he re-explains to us what really happened:

for example, that Afghanistan wasn't always a Muslim country; it was conquered by Arabs, but in the beginning, they were Buddhists. And when he's not sure about something, he asks Zaher. Zaher knows the history of his country really well—way better than we know our own, anyway. His grandfather taught him all about it when he was little. He says it's different from the official history that they started teaching when the Taliban came into power. He often tells us about it, bit by bit, and we all listen. One day, Zaher brought in an old map of his country; it was folded

into tiny squares and super beat-up. We helped him tape it all up and then we put it on the wall beside the blackboard.

So anyway, that day we were talking about Baghdad.

Mr. Lopez was telling us about the legend of the Round City, which is also called the City of al-Mansur, or the City of Peace. He described its four gates, its mosque, where people worshipped, and its shining dome.

All of a sudden we hear a murmur in the school; it rises toward us and swells through the hallways. The sounds of the voices rush into our class. They say, "It's the police." They say, "It's a raid." They say, "It's the drug squad."

The door opens, and police in uniforms burst into the room. They go to the back and sides of the class, encircling us; they're armed. A man comes in with a dog, a muzzled German shepherd that he's holding on a leash. Mr. Lopez steps in front of him and puts up his hands, trying to

slow him down. He asks what's
going on, who are they, what are they
doing. The highest-ranking one in-
terrupts him; he's the sergeant. "Quiet!
This is a police operation. Nobody
move, nobody leave their seats!" I'm
not listening to him; I'm watching the
dog. He's starting to sniff around.

▬▬▬ ●

Paradise is really quiet, normally. It's
not the ghetto.

It's a funny name, anyway. Paradise
Heights. It's not a town or a suburb,

just an area of the city. There are stores, a movie theater, a library, our school: Paradise School, the largest in the city, from kindergarten up to grade twelve. Once in a while some gangs of guys get in a fight near the park, but other than that it's totally calm. There are no cars on fire or shattered store windows, and they don't talk about us on the news; honestly, it's a normal neighborhood. It's not paradise either, but it's nice. Sometimes cops go by on patrol, but they rarely arrest anyone.

And now, there are police wagons

under our windows, all along the
sidewalk up to the intersection.
They're blocking the whole avenue,
people are stopping, drivers are slow-
ing down trying to see what's going
on. There's even a helicopter circling
above us. You bet we're going to see
this tonight on TV!

▬▬▬ ●

I know what the dog is for; I know
why he's here.

The man with the dog looks just like
his dog. No, actually, he's uglier than

his dog. The dog sniffs around, but once in a while, he stops. He looks like he's fed up; he probably wishes they'd just leave him in peace. But the guy with the dog, he never stops. He won't let the dog rest; he takes off the muzzle, tightens the leash around his neck, makes him sniff again, encourages him, gets him worked up. Of the two, he's more of a dog.

Mr. Lopez rummages around in his binder. An officer tells him not to touch anything. Mr. Lopez shows him his cellphone. The officer comes

toward him. "You can't use your phone. You can't call anyone."

Mr. Lopez answers, "It's not a personal call. I just have to advise the principal." He starts pressing the number.

The policeman grabs his wrist and shouts, "You put down that phone, did you hear me? You're not calling anyone!"

Mr. Lopez cries out, "Come on, are you nuts?" He turns to the sergeant. "Please, tell this man to let me go!"

The sergeant answers, "You can't call your principal. Anyway, she already knows what's happening."

━━ ●

My dad is a police officer, too. He might even work with these guys.

Not long ago, my dad came into our class to give a lecture on drug prevention. He told us about all the categories of drugs and the dangers to your health and about the law and the risks if you break it. He used a computer to show slides. Jesus, these cops

know more about drugs than we do.

I was so embarrassed. Since my mom started working as a teacher here, that's already given me a reputation. The last thing I need is to be the class narc.

My dad kept glancing at me out of the corner of his eye during his presentation, trying to look casual. I don't think he thought I noticed. This stuff is so important to him. I really hope he doesn't suspect anything; if he finds out I smoke, he'll scalp me. I remember when I got my dreadlocks—he turned green.

He's always calm. Too calm. It makes me nervous. He speaks in a solemn voice, projecting quiet strength—the wise man with everything under control. But I know him; inside, he's boiling. He's the opposite of my mom. She's more like "I'll warn you once, but the second time, I'll punish you." I'm the same way, except that I'll punish you straight off. My dad's the opposite of us: he warns, he re-warns, he triple warns. All he knows is how to warn; he never punishes. I don't know how he ever became a police officer.

My dad says that cops are there to protect us. That the police aren't against us but with us, serving the citizens. That at school we should feel safe. When he says that, I laugh; I tell him he sounds like a politician and it's just nice words. The truth is that their job is to make us shit our pants as much as possible. That always gets him worked up and we get into a fight.

I don't know what it is with me— ever since I was little, I get angry really quickly. It happens just like that: I'm calm, and then all of a sudden I

explode. I pound on the walls, the doors, everything... My parents took me to see a shrink and he said I was having tantrums. Oh really, you think? Then, he added that it was because of my parents, because they represent "double authority figures": police officer and teacher. Yeah, no kidding. "Why are you hassling *me*, then?" I yelled at him, and then I left.

On the whole my folks are pretty decent, I have to admit, but there are two or three things they never stop hassling me about. There were already the tantrums, and then lately, they've

been bugging me about what I'm going to do with my life. That's what they're obsessed with right now, so it makes for some fun conversations around the dinner table.

"So, what do you want to do when you're finished school? Do you have any plans?"

"No, I don't know anything! Obviously you knew at seven years old that you were going to be a cop until you die, but I'm not like you!"

"First of all, you're going to stop talking to me that way and, next,

you're going to stop being stupid. You have to stop saying the first nasty thing that passes through your head and think about it instead, because you're anything but stupid."

"Fine, what do you want me to say? I don't know what I want to do!"

"You have the right not to know, but tell us at least that you'll go see the guidance counselor."

"God, it's my life and you're the ones who are worried about it! What do you want to guide me to, then? I don't want your counselor. I don't need it.

I have Mr. Lopez, who answers our questions when we have them. There, that's what I want to be: a history teacher. Does that make you feel better?"

"Okay, why not, but then maybe you need to work a little harder in history..."

I didn't reply; sometimes I don't even have the strength to keep arguing.

▬▬●

I have a bag of weed hidden in my

pocket. It's not very much, but it's enough. The dog comes right toward me; he sniffs around my desk and starts to whimper. His tail whips my legs and he slobbers on my shoes. He comes up onto me and nibbles at my thighs. The guy with the dog lets him dirty my things for a little longer and then he takes my bag. I'm scared he'll break my camera.

I clench my fists; I know what's going to happen. The others look at me. I don't want to meet their gazes. Yes, I smoke; everyone knows it. It's people like me they're looking for;

there, they found me. I'll go with
them and the rest of the class will
sigh in relief, this time. That's how it
is; that's the game, I knew it from
the start. It's not exactly reassuring
to know, but I'm not surprised. The
dog grabs my shirt and pulls on it;
the sleeve rips; I try to protect myself
but the cop says to me, "Don't move
or he'll rip off your kneecap!"

He makes me get up and I'm about
to follow him when the dog gives a
strangled yap. All of a sudden he
burrows his nose into Zaher's
sweater. I smoked next to him after

lunch. His clothes smell like the joint. The dog growls, showing his teeth; Zaher looks terrified. He doesn't like dogs very much, and I'm the only one who knows why. A cop grabs him, and without thinking, I say, "Wait, he didn't do anything."

The other one pushes on my back. "Quiet! Both of you, follow us."

In the hallway there are cops everywhere, on guard in front of the open doors, holding their guns. Machine guns. I know that model; it's an MP5, the same as my dad's. In front of each class there are little groups like ours,

separated from the rest of their class-
mates. I see Patrick, Harith, Ismael,
Jerome, Mike, and some others I don't
know. There are a few girls in a sepa-
rate group, and some female cops are
leading them away.

They make us go down into the
courtyard, and then make us all line
up at the back, noses against the
wall, with our bags behind us. We're
not allowed to turn around. A dog
goes by to sniff the bags, slowly. I
feel someone pat me down; I try to
look back over my shoulder but I
can't see anything. Once he's finished,

we're allowed to turn around. Someone comes by and asks us for our full
names and addresses. He writes everything down on a list, then he leaves.

We stay like this. It's funny; there's
no noise, no screams, no slamming
doors, or broken glass, or shoving
against the wall. Just silence. The atmosphere is strange—I don't know,
muffled; there are no sounds of life
from the school. The only sound, now
and then, is the deafening racket of a
helicopter flying over the courtyard.
After a while it gets farther away and
it doesn't come back.

Mr. Lopez and the other teachers have disappeared. I try to look for my mother, but I don't see her. At one point the principal walks by us, quickly, not looking at us, talking on the phone. The sound of her high heels echoes for a long time between the courtyard walls.

It's cold. My stomach hurts. All we're doing is standing here. No one comes to see us or talk to us. Zaher is looking for his *pakol* in his pocket; the cops point at him with their guns and tell him to pull out his hands. He lifts them above his head;

they laugh and tell him to lower them.

I want so badly to get out my camera and take pictures of everything. Instead, I take pictures in my head. *Click*, the butt of the rifle that's a bit scuffed. *Click*, the cop picking his nose. *Click*, the black clouds drifting slowly across the sky.

Finally, they take us inside.

They lead us into the cafeteria. They make the cooks and cleaning ladies leave, pushing them outside. They didn't have time to finish cleaning;

the floor is disgusting. It's the first time I've been in here outside of lunchtime; we sure don't make their job easy.

A cop claps his hands. "Okay, everybody strip off your clothes!" We look at each other; nobody moves. "Come on! Everybody take off your clothes and put them in front of you! Let's go! Those who understand can translate for the others; we're not going to repeat it in Arab or Bamboola!"

We take off our clothes in silence. When we get down to our boxers, we hesitate; they don't really want us

to get totally naked? We look at each other, and look at the cops, questioning them with our eyes. They look back without a word. Finally I say, "Sir, do we really have to take off everything?"

The cop laughs. "What do you think?"

"Well, I don't know," I say.

The cop plants himself in front of me. "You can stay as you are. We've seen enough, we're not animals."

There's a young cop. While his bud-

dies are rummaging through our clothes, he's supposed to keep an eye on us. He can hardly look at us anymore. When they brought us in here, he was yelling at us just like all the others. Now that we're standing in front of him undressed, he's looking away. He looks embarrassed to be the only one in the room wearing clothes.

I'm shaking from my head to my toes, shitting myself. I don't want to show them that I'm scared, but I can't seem to help it. My nose is running and I have nothing to wipe it. I blow

my nose, everything spraying out onto the floor. The cop says, "Hey, where do you think you are, you think it's not dirty enough here?" I wipe my nose with my fingers. I rub them together so they dry, but my nose won't stop running.

I keep shooting photos in silence. *Click*, the cops' studded boots shining under the fluorescent lights. *Click*, my friends in their underwear: skinny Zaher, fat Harith, muscular Jerome.

They turn over our clothes and pull at them. Some of them rip. The dog slobbers on them. Then they throw

them back on the ground, with the mixture of lunch remains and shoe dirt. At the end there's one big, messy pile in the middle of the cafeteria—bags, pants, sneakers. Other classes are going down into the courtyard; they watch us through the cafeteria windows as we go find our clothes and put them back on.

Two cops come back in, followed by the sergeant. They look at their list. They call out, "Zaher Arash?" Zaher lowers his eyes and raises his hand. "Zaher Arash, that's you?" Zaher nods yes. "Answer us, are you Zaher Arash?"

"Yes, sir."

"Follow us."

I go to hold him back; he shakes his head at me. The sergeant sees me. He says, "Are you Martin Leduc?"

I look at him and take my time replying, "That's me, sir."

He has a bizarre smile. He says, "You're coming, too."

They take us into the admin offices, another place where we never normally go. The sergeant wedges his ass into the principal's chair and

plugs a laptop in above the printer.
We stay standing in front of him,
with the other two cops behind us.
They close the door.

I have a bad feeling—why did they
bring just the two of us into this office, away from the others? My eyes
search the room. There's a door at
the back; I take a mental picture of it.
The sound of a dial-up Internet
connection comes from the laptop.
I take more silent pictures: the pale
light from the screen on the sergeant's
face, the framed photo of the principal's kids sitting on the shelf.

The bell rings for recess on the other side of the wall, in the younger kids' courtyard. The noises come back; we can faintly hear children laughing, yelling, running. It's strange, usually the little brats annoy me, shrieking like a bunch of birds, but today it makes me feel better to hear them. It gives me courage.

The sergeant looks at us for a long time, then starts reading a piece of paper out of the printer, as if we weren't even there. Zaher keeps his eyes lowered.

I speak. "Excuse me, sir, why are the

two of us here?"

He smiles at me again, but it's only his mouth smiling; the rest of his face is frozen.

"You're Martin Leduc?"

"I already told you that, sir."

"Then say it again."

"That's me, sir."

"You're the son of Bernard Leduc?"

"Yes, sir."

"Police Chief Leduc?"

"Yes, sir."

Silence.

"Your dad will be happy when we tell him what we found on you. Don't you think?"

"No… But this has nothing to do with my dad, sir. And it has nothing to do with him, he doesn't even smoke," I add, pointing to Zaher.

"That's what you say," the sergeant says with his little smile. "Well, guess what, your friend here, not only does he not have the right to be here but

his family has asked for political asylum. We came here looking for dealers, and we found illegals. You're going to tell me that you didn't know that either?"

"Well... No."

"And why do you think he became your friend?"

"How do you know he's my friend?"

"Several students in your class say that he spends a lot of time with you. Maybe his parents think it will help their case, if they have connections

with the family of a police officer…
Unless it was his idea?"

I turn toward Zaher; he lifts his head
suddenly. I fix his eyes with mine, and
he shakes his head *no*. The sergeant
takes his sheet of paper again. He
looks at Zaher but without smiling
this time.

"Zaher Arash, born April 29, 1992.
Afghan nationality. Father's name
Ahmad Arash. That's correct?"

"Yes, sir."

"You fled from Pakistan. Why?"

"Because we were in danger."

"You were wanted?"

"No, sir. We were chased."

"Chased? What did you do to get chased?"

"Nothing."

"Don't say nothing! There's got to be a reason."

"No."

"You planted bombs?"

"That's a lie! We don't have bombs

in my family and we're from Afghanistan!"

The cop behind Zaher smacks him on the head and knocks off his cap. "You, lower your eyes for a start, and then answer the sergeant politely!"

Zaher's face is on fire. He bends down to pick up his cap but he keeps it held tightly in his hands, as if he wants to tear it. My thoughts are racing. What's going on here?

The interrogator continues.

"Why did you come to this country?"

"Because my grandfather, he came here once a long time ago, I think."

"What did you do in Afghanistan?"

"Huh?"

"Your father. What did he do?"

"He was a journalist."

"And your grandfather?"

"Musician."

"They were in the war?"

"Just my grandfather."

"It's because of him that you fled the country?"

"No, it's my dad."

"Your dad, why your dad?"

"He wrote articles…"

"Shut up!" I tell him. "They don't have the right to ask you these questions. They're not responsible for your immigration file."

The cop smacks the back of my head. The sergeant gestures to him to stop. He thinks for a moment. He makes a little sign to the two cops. One

rummages through our bags again, and the other takes our fingerprints. Then they tell us to undress, and we can tell by their tone that this time, they mean everything. While they search our clothes, we wait, hands over our cocks. One of them puts on gloves and searches through my hair. He pulls on my dreads, one after the other. Then he makes us bend forward and we have to cough while he shines a flashlight up our assholes.

When it's over, the sergeant plants himself in front of Zaher and holds my bag of weed under his nose. "We

found this in your bag. It's not enough that you come to our country, you come here to sell this shit?"

I shout, "No one deals in our class, sir! Especially not him! You found it in my pocket!"

He turns to me.

"Go on, Leduc, keep talking! With your attitude, this dope, and your family relations, you're really up the creek!"

I go quiet.

I think I'm starting to understand his game. He wants to use the weed

first to pressure my father by threatening to accuse me of trafficking, and second to deport Zaher by accusing him of the same thing.

My dad has a reputation in his squad as an honest cop. He always says that police work is a public service. Police can't do whatever they want, they have responsibilities to people. The use of force is a last resort, not a solution. That makes some of the other cops grind their teeth. Not everyone thinks like him, although there are more and

more lately who do, and even some of the most stubborn ones are starting to come around. Some of them are even starting to refuse orders to bring up the number of arrests. The problem is, there's always someone else willing to play dirty.

We get dressed while the sergeant uses the phone in the office next door. He comes back. He says to me, "I didn't get your father, but with the message I left him, he should be here soon. Then we'll have a little discussion."

Then he asks Zaher, "Your sister is

at the Paradise kindergarten?" But he doesn't wait for an answer. "We've gone to get her; you're going to come with us to your parents' place."

With those words, Zaher explodes. He springs toward the door with a howl. I grab him to keep him from leaving, but the two cops react in an instant. They're on us before we even touch the door. The bigger one pushes Zaher to the ground and twists his arms behind his back.

I yell, "He's not going to run away, he's not going to run away! Stop hurting him!"

The other one holds me back. His arm is across my neck. I'm strangled, I can't speak. He pulls me back and pushes me into a chair. I feel hand-cuffs around my wrists. He won't let me go. I can't breathe, my ears are buzzing. I see everything, but I can't hear anything.

I faintly make out Zaher's cries through the confusion. The big cop tries to shut him up by hitting him in the sides. Finally Zaher huddles up to protect himself and goes silent. He stays on the ground, moaning, rolled up into a ball. The cop pulls

out a black plastic strap. He winds it around Zaher's wrists and pulls it tight, with a sudden jerk. Then he pulls him up by the strap and pushes his face down on the desk. He keeps him that way, his nose in the papers, while he questions him. Zaher speaks in a rasp, his breath cut off.

"For the last time, you don't know what you're doing in our country?"

"No, sir."

"Bombs, beards, all that, you don't know about it?"

"I don't know what you're talking about, sir."

"So, you're not the ones who make women wear veils? You're not the ones who stone them, huh? Well, don't worry, we'll send you back to your country of fanatics. We'll see what they do to you there; you'll wish you were back in this country!"

Fuck you, you big asshole, I scream in my head. *Afghanistan was already an empire when our ancestors hardly knew how to start a fire! Fuck you, you and this country of assholes. If this is my country, I don't want anything to do with it!*

I'm sweating. I'm fighting the words boiling in my head, fighting so I won't let them out, because I know if I do, it's Zaher who will pay the price. I try to concentrate on other things— on the pain in my wrists, on the weight of my body in the chair, on the sweat dripping down my neck. I tell myself that each drop of sweat is an insult that escapes instead of a word. I speak to myself in my head so I won't speak out loud. I speak to Zaher in secret so that nobody will hear us.

Your name is Zaher. It's the name of

the last king of your country. Your country is called Afghanistan. That means "country of Afghans," that's the Persian name that they gave to Pashtuns. You were born April 29, 1992, in Kabul. The day of the rebel victory over the Taliban. Your grandfather fought with the Mujahideen in the Northern Alliance and went into the government that drove the Taliban out. But the fighting never stopped. The Taliban were supported by the Pakistani army. When the Taliban took back power four years later, they hunted down the president and the ministers. They caught your

grandfather. They hung him from a stoplight with metal wire.

Your father's newspaper was banned and his office was set on fire. They looked for your family, too, because of his articles. You fled to the north, where you hid in a village in Badakhshan. When you were nine years old, soldiers with dogs attacked the village; they let the dogs loose on you, and then they burned everything, and they burned your hair, too. You crossed into Pakistan just before the Americans arrived. The Taliban regime fell in 2001, but the war continued.

Because your father wrote as much
against the Americans as he did
against the Taliban or the Russians,
you couldn't go back to Afghanistan.
He kept writing and you kept hiding.
And then he got sick and this year,
you came here.

That's your story. I'm the only one
who knows it like that.

━━ ●

The daylight starts to fade outside.
Zaher's little sister walks across the
courtyard flanked by two cops. She's

crying, alone in the growing darkness. The voices of the children next door have disappeared.

When she sees Zaher, she throws herself into his arms. He speaks to her softly in Pashtun. She calms down. The police make a sign to him to go.

In the doorway, Zaher turns toward me. He says, "*Djur Baashi.*" "Stay fresh"—it's an expression in Dari. He takes off his *pakol* and puts it in my hands. Then he gives me a last look, as if he's trying to reassure me. I must really look like a wreck for him to look at me that way. The cop

pushes on his back.

I'm suffocating again, it's like the air has left my body. When I get my voice back, I yell, "*Zenda Baashi, Zenda Baashi!*" It means "Stay alive." The sergeant slams the door. I press my face to the window; I see them one last time, him from the back with his little yellow cap, his sister clinging to his shoulder. I force myself to smile at him but they've already disappeared into the black, no turning around. I stare into the black, the black, the black until they pull me away, toward the police van.

▬▬ ●

I spent the night in custody, in a cell smelling of piss and disinfectant. The disinfectant was worse than the piss.

They brought me there, together with Moussa, Patrick, Harith, and some others. They took our identification and fingerprints, they photographed us. We waited, handcuffed to a bench, in the hall. The police station looked like it had been totally renovated—it shone under the new light fixtures, and the people who passed us made *squeak, squeak* noises with their shoes.

I tried to take more mental pictures, but I couldn't. There was nothing to see.

They separated us for interrogation. I found myself face to face with the cop who hit Zaher. He tapped away on his computer for a bit, then told me to sign the statement about my questioning. It said that I resisted the forces of law, that I compromised a police operation with my aggressive behavior. I pushed the pen away. I said it wasn't the truth, and for starters, the pot was in my pocket and not Zaher's. He looked exasperated and cracked his knuckles.

I felt a cold sweat on my back but I couldn't stop myself. Without leaving him time to answer, I asked if I could use the phone. He said it was too late, but I could call in the morning. I said that I wanted to call my parents. He smiled and said, "If that's what you're worried about, they already know."

I asked where Zaher was. He said that he didn't know. I asked why he wasn't with us. He said that was police headquarters' business. I asked, "Will he be deported?"

He said, "You're not going to see him again."

I said, "Why did you hit him? You don't even know him!"

He said, "I hit who I want, and I don't give a shit about your buddy. Now shut up and sign."

I took a deep breath. I picked up the pen and I started to write. "My name is Zaher Arash I'm an Afghan refugee I fled the war in my country of origin and now in the country where I live I'm the victim of forces of law who have compromised a police operation with their aggressive behavior..."

When he understood what I was doing, he ripped the sheet away from me and started to read it. I continued speaking out loud. I was hoping there was a microphone hidden somewhere. "My name is Zaher Arash. I am not a drug trafficker. I'm a student in grade twelve at Paradise School. My best subjects are language and history, and also art…"

With a swift kick he sent my chair flying against the radiator. He grabbed me by the neck. Two other cops entered and held him back from hitting me. Another threw me into the room

next door. He said, "You're going to spend the night with us; that will make you think!"

He took off my shoelaces and belt before locking me in. The cell was new, too. Everything was gray—the walls, the bed, the table, the door. The only spot of color was Zaher's hat, sitting on the bed. The area around the toilet smelled like piss, everything else smelled like disinfectant. It was an hour before my body stopped trembling and my breathing calmed down.

They brought me supper. It looked

like the stuff that the meal service
delivers to my grandmother. I didn't
eat anything, anyway. My gut hurt
and my head ached. I felt beaten up
all over, as if I had been in a boxing
match. I fell on my knees and vomited
for I don't know how long; I didn't
think my body could even hold that
much stuff. After, I felt empty inside,
emptied of everything, cleansed,
drained of strength.

They brought me a blanket. My legs
wouldn't hold me up any longer; I
curled into a ball and spent the rest
of the night shivering.

━━ ●

My parents didn't come to get me until the morning.

It wasn't the same cops as before who brought me out of the cell. I was like a zombie. A woman made me sit in her office, and I hardly understood what she was telling me. She glanced at me, then quickly lowered her eyes to her papers. "You were brought here by the intervention squad? They're not exactly gentle. You can't blame them, it's not always easy…"

Then she explained that I was taken

in for possession of an illegal sub-
stance and for disobeying the orders
of police. She said that I would go to
trial, and she made me sign a paper.
Finally she told me that my parents
were there and that I could go home
while awaiting the trial.

I followed another cop. He asked me
if I wanted to use the toilet. I said
no. He gave me back my belt and
shoelaces, and I stuffed them in my
pocket. The only thing I wanted was
to get out of there.

My mom looked like she had aged
ten years. My dad was white with

rage. He spoke with a trembling voice. He wanted to take my arm but I pulled away. We left as the other cops saluted him respectfully.

━━ ●

I managed to get news of Zaher, but it was too late.

They drove Zaher and his sister back to their place. They woke up Zaher's father and arrested him. He was asleep because he worked night shifts and slept during the day. Zaher had to translate what the cops were saying.

Then his mother came home, and they took all four of them to a detention center. They kept them there overnight, then the next day they sent them to Afghanistan.

As soon as Zaher was taken away, some of the teachers alerted an association that defends the rights of immigrants. The people from the association tried to trace Zaher's family, but all the services were shutting down for the day. When they found out that they were at the detention center, they called and were told that the family was there, but they weren't able to

speak to them. The next morning, around the same time I was getting out of jail, the association people went to the center and learned that the family had just been taken to the airport.

━━ ●

The night after I got out of jail, a cop car on patrol was pelted with rocks in front of the school. They sent reinforcements, and within fifteen minutes it was war. Harith called me—he lives just across the street from the school—and said, "Come

on! We're going to give it to the cops!"
I snuck out the window. I got there
right when the riot police vans were
pulling up in front of the school. We
bombarded them with rocks, cans,
garbage overflowing from the
Dumpsters—we didn't think about
it, we just threw whatever we could
find. There were some kids from
school, and some others that none of
us recognized. Some of them were
wearing scarves or hoods. All of a
sudden there was a flash, like a fire-
cracker exploding right beside me,
and the next second a car parked
along the street was on fire. I stopped

and caught my breath; I couldn't take my eyes off the twisting flames. Then we heard a whistle and the cops charged. I started running straight ahead, I heard the cries behind my back, I didn't stop. The light from the flames disappeared, the noises faded away. I kept running through the deserted streets. It was cold; my lungs burned in my chest, I kept running. I ended up at an unfamiliar intersection; all the lights were flashing yellow, and there wasn't a car in sight. I turned around and I didn't recognize anything. My lungs let out a funny high-pitched whistling sound;

it hurt. I lay down on the ground and I stayed there.

I think I fell asleep because the next thing I heard was a very loud car engine sound, and when I opened my eyes I was blinded by the headlights of a car speeding by me. I got up and followed one of the roads, and when I got to the end, I recognized where I was. I had practically made a tour of the city. I walked home, holding on to the walls so I wouldn't fall down. I didn't go back by the school, I didn't pass anyone. All the lights were still out at my place. I slid back

in the window, being super careful
not to make any noise. I asked myself
if it was all a dream before collapsing
onto my bed.

━━ ●

The police wouldn't say where
Zaher's family was deported to. They
confirmed that there were no official
charges against them, not drug trafficking or anything. They were just
undocumented immigrants on foreign
soil. They were taken back to the
border according to the directives of
the minister of the interior. The

ministry had applied "extradition procedures," they said.

The cops called them illegals, but that wasn't true. Everyone knew where they lived, what kind of work they did, what school they went to… they just didn't have their papers, that's all. This whole thing was all about papers. And now their request for asylum was canceled, and their file was destroyed.

Since they left, I don't eat anymore, I don't sleep; I spend my time thinking of them, wondering where they might be. I take tons of imaginary photos

in my head, but they just erase themselves right away; I'm too exhausted to do it. I have dreams that mix what really happened with the images I saw on TV—I don't know anymore what's real and what's not. I don't leave my room. I keep up with things through my parents, the radio, the TV, the telephone, but I don't have the courage to go outside. I'm afraid the cops will take me back to school, to prison, or to who knows where.

And them? Where are they now? I try to accompany them in my thoughts: the cities of Kabul, Herat, Kandahar,

Jalalabad… I wish I was there. I don't feel at home here anymore. I feel like an illegal, too. The truth is, from one day to another, we're all illegals.

I was right, our school did end up on TV, but they mostly showed cops who said that the operation was carried out smoothly. The sergeant said that because of the extraordinary collaboration between the forces of law and the education department, several arrests allowed them to dismantle a drug-trafficking network

with international connections. We saw the front of the school, with two cops standing there, and no noise inside. Did they film just the beginning, or what?

After that we saw the principal sitting at her desk, everything put back in order. There was no trace that we had been there. She explained that she had asked for the intervention and that it was the logical next step from the previous drug prevention initiatives. The goal was to protect the students.

Then, it was the crown prosecutor's

turn. His office was even more luxurious. He talked very slowly, enunciating each word carefully. He said there was nothing worse in adolescents than a sense of impunity—that school was not a zone outside the law.

Then the TV showed a tiny, messy office. It was the office of the representative of the teachers' union. He denounced the intrusion of the police into an area filled with very young students. He talked about preserving the integrity of educational establishments.

Right after that we saw the sergeant

again. He wasn't as calm as at the beginning. He was mocking the accusations of some liberal-thinking people who condemn police brutality, but when it's their kids being preyed upon by foreign drug dealers, they're the first to ask the police to intervene.

The two ministers of justice and education looked uncomfortable when the news cameras caught them leaving a nice restaurant. It seems they will "initiate an inquiry" into the incident.

While I was watching the TV screen, I surprised myself by shooting mental pictures again. It was like a tic. Only

now, I was taking images of the images on TV. I told myself, you're nuts, so I got my camera and took some real shots: the prosecutor with his slicked-back hair, all the journalists pushing their microphones at the ministers, the anchorwoman with her cleavage —not too much, not too little.

The next story came on, and she switched to her Serious Look Number 12 to announce the number of American soldiers killed in Iraq.

▬▬●

My mom was at an appointment the day of the drug raid, and she told me when she got to school that afternoon, everything was cordoned off. She told them that she was a teacher and her son was a student inside, but they refused to let her pass. On order of the principal, they said: no one goes in, no one goes out. There were lots of parents waiting for their little kids. My mom said she gave the guards at the entrance the lecture of their life.

The day after the raid, the teachers and school staff went on strike. They showed Mr. Lopez speaking in front

of the school on the local news. I had never seen him so worked up. He denounced the raid and explained what had happened to Zaher and his family.

The teachers' union and parents' association wrote to the politicians to protest against the police methods. Together with the immigrant defense associations and human rights groups, they filed a complaint against Zaher's deportation. It was dismissed.

Not everyone at the school went on strike. My mom said they argued about it in the teachers' lounge.

Some of them thought the raid was
justified. The math teacher said it
would teach us respect, and called
her a socialist or hippie or something
like that. She was so mad when she
told us about it that I was afraid to
interrupt her. Anyway, I didn't want
to talk about it too much, because
we had a harsh discussion over the
drugs and I felt a bit sick about it.

▬ ●

It's all I talk about now with my
friends. When we all saw each other
again, it was just before the trial. They

thought I knew about Zaher's illegal status and that I had hidden it from them.

"Asshole, you should have told us."

"Yeah, if we knew, we would have protected him!"

"Did you see the way those pigs looked at us? You'd think that they were afraid of us!"

"But they're all afraid of us! The teachers, the police, our parents— afraid that we won't come to school, that we'll break the rules, that we won't get career counseling…"

"They're bugging you about the counseling, too?"

"Shit, they won't stop about their counseling…"

"I know, if I don't follow their hundred-year career plan, they think I'll end up a delinquent on welfare bringing shame to my family…"

"They freak out too much. The truth is, they're the ones who scare me!"

━━ •

The trial happened quickly; I thought

it would take a lot longer. We were all with our families at the courthouse, in a big room where they judged us one after the other, ten minutes each. I couldn't bring in my camera. I tried again to take pictures in my head, but it didn't work.

The prosecutor was the guy I saw on TV. He still had his hair slicked back. He talked to me without looking at me, making lots of gestures. He wasn't as controlled as he looked on TV. He said that I was more responsible for my actions than the others because I was the son of a police officer, that I

understood the gravity of my acts, and that I had encouraged the others to resist.

My parents had found me a lawyer. The guy wasn't exactly a laugh, but he was nice. We talked for a long time to prepare for the trial, and he remembered everything I told him. At last, someone who listened. He defended me well, even if he slanted the truth a bit: average but serious student, civil servant parents, adolescent rebelling against authority, used a small amount of drugs once in a while. He said that I was the target

of false accusations of trafficking. He added that my parents had filed a complaint of violence against the police.

The judge was pretty old and wrinkled. She talked in a calm voice; you could tell that she was the boss. One time the prosecutor cut her off, and she shot him down without even raising her voice. He hardly dared to open his mouth after that. Compared to her, even Mr. Lopez had no authority!

While the prosecutor talked, the judge read my file as if she were alone in her office. But when my lawyer started, the judge lifted her

eyes toward me, over the top of her little glasses. She looked me straight in the eyes. She looked super severe, but I could see there was no meanness in her eyes.

In the end, I got a suspended sentence and a fine, and I didn't get sent back to the piss and disinfectant. There were others who weren't so lucky. Harith was sent to jail, and Jerome, too.

▬ ●

And then my dad had some problems.

It must have really been bugging him because he didn't talk about it, not even to my mom. The pressure from my arrest wasn't enough to force him to resign, but it seemed like his career was over anyway. He said he wanted to quit. He was fed up.

He said to me, "I'm sorry that a minority of police officers give our law enforcement the image of a band of thugs, and our government the image of fascists."

I said, "Can you repeat that more slowly?"

He acted like he didn't hear me. He said, "I'm sorry."

I said, "Why are you sorry? You didn't do anything; it's me, it's my fault!"

He shouted, "No, no, no!"

My mother intervened. "Why are you saying that, Martin?"

"Well, if I hadn't smoked next to him, they would never have checked him and he would still be here."

My dad shook his head. "Look, they were on borrowed time anyway. Their

file was pending at police headquarters; it was just a matter of time until they were deported."

"So, what, there was nothing that could have been done?"

"Not really, no. It's the law."

"So, to you, it's fine what happened?"

"How can you say that? Are you blind? Don't you see what we've been through?"

"Wait, that was because I was there. But if it had just happened to Zaher, would you have done the same?"

They looked at each other, and my mom finished by saying, "Yes, I think that we would have spoken up anyway. Legal citizen or not, no kid deserves to be treated that way."

"Either way, I'm not a citizen anymore!"

My dad put his hand on my arm. "Yes, you are. If you say that, you let them win, you become powerless, too. If things like this happen, it's because the law is not right, and it's citizens who can change it."

I didn't answer, but I didn't pull my arm away.

Today I go back to school.

I still have that word bouncing around in my head: *illegal.* I may not know what that means exactly, but I know one thing: I want to see Zaher again. And after that, I don't know, but I'll find out. And without a guidance counselor, either. The first thing I'll do is learn Pashtun, but properly— the whole language, not just the swear words. And as soon as I know it, I'll leave for Afghanistan. I'll leave to find him.

I don't have many clues—just what I know about his history, his family, the map he gave us, and then the only photo I have of him, the one I took. I'll have to find out the rest on my own.

I'll bring my camera so I won't have to take photos in my head. I'll take them for real, without hiding. I'll do that as a job—photographer. Or maybe history teacher. Or journalist, maybe, but not for TV. I haven't decided. All I know is, I'll never be a cop.

But that's all for later.

I'm going back to school, and everyone will be watching me. I'm going back to Paradise, the biggest school in the city, but I'm still alone. I'm going back and I'm scared.

It's my fault.

Single Voice

Single Voice

Single Voice